THE GREAT BIG MOVE

A SURPRISINGLY EXCITING ADVENTURE

written by Meghan Marie Geary

illustrated by Brooke O'Neill

THIS BOOK BELONGS TO

The Great Big Move: A Surprisingly Exciting Adventure ©
First Printing, 2018 in the United States of America
Text and Art copyright © 2018 Meghan Marie Geary
ISBN-13: 978-1725068131
ISBN-10: 1725068133

www.meghanmariegeary.com

To my girls, Karsyn and Hartlyn, this story is for
you, to remind you that life is an adventure!
Everything happens for a reason so enjoy it all!
Fill your mind with wonder not worry, find those silver
linings in every situation and paint your path with it,
leaving that little bit of sparkle wherever you go!
Thank you for making my path shine brighter,
I love you more than anything in this world.

Adventure awaits my girls!

Remember to always be kind, be confident, be positive
and present but most importantly always BE YOU!

To Tim, thank you for making this adventure possible. ♥

Hi there! My name is Katie Harlow. I'm seven years old.
My favorite color is purple! I love all things rainbows,
unicorns and sharks—yes, sharks!

So, I think the most perfect animal in the whole wide world
is a Narwhal. (It's pretty much a unicorn shark!)

I have one sister, a mama and a daddy. I love my family!

Did you know I have lived in two different states and have had three different homes already!?

I know, in just my seven short years that's a lot! My family has to move a lot.

Have you ever moved before?

A lot of my friends have never, ever moved before. They even live in the same town as their cousins and grandparents because even THEY have never moved before. I think that is so totally cool!!

I live pretty far from all of my big family. But when I visit them or they visit me it's almost like we are having one big party! It is such a special occasion and that is pretty awesome and so fun!!

You know what else?
My Grandma and Grandpa
even make a special phone
call that's just for me every
week (that makes me
feel pretty cool).

Well anyways... I have some news. Mama and Daddy sat me and my sissy down and said Daddy was given a...

uh... what's that word again?

A PREGOTION or a PRENOTION?

No, no—**PROMOTION** was the word!
I guess it means Daddy has a new job.

They said it's a good thing, so that makes me happy!
Mama and Daddy said we will be starting a great
new adventure! I do love going on adventures!

S.S. HARLOW

But the thing is, Daddy's new job is in a new place.
Do you know what that means?

I have to move.
Which means I have
to leave my friends,
my school, my house,
and my room.

And my soccer team
and dance studio, too.

Oh man, and that really cool park that looks like a castle and that hill mama drives down and we all put our hands in the air and scream like it's a roller coaster.

I really love all of these things. Ugh, and I am really going to miss them!

When I moved last time I remember missing my friends and the apartment we lived in. I really missed the pool we used to swim in, too.

Oh yeah, and that donut shop mama would walk
my sissy and me to for breakfast.

Ugh, that was hard. I was sad and I missed all of that stuff.

But you know what's kinda cool?!?!
Now that I've been at my new (well, almost old now) home, I still get to talk to my old friends!

I write them letters and
even go visit them.
It is so fun!!

KATIE HARLOW
JOHN

My friends think
it's pretty cool that
I have friends in a
different state.
(I do too!)

Meeting new friends is a little scary. I wish this adventure had some kind of map to tell me where to find them!

How did I meet all of my other friends?

Mama always told me on the way to school, "Be you today, Katie Harlow, always be you." I listened. (I don't always listen.)

Sometimes, I would sit by myself or play alone at recess. On those days I would feel a little sad.

Then I would call my old friends or play with my family when I got home to cheer me up.

But there were other days where I wasn't alone. I just kept being myself and I started making new friends I would play with or sit with. Now they are the friends I'm going to come back and visit! Just like my old friends I go and visit!

Holy moly, that's two states I'm going to have friends in!
This is awesome!! Wowzers, I wonder who I will meet next?!?

Wait a second... I just thought of something.

If I had never moved away from my first old friends and the pool and the donut shop, I never would have found my new friends or gotten to play at the castle park or drive down the roller coaster hill with my hands up!! Gosh, it would be sad if I had never discovered those.

DONUTS

You know what? I'm glad we found those things!

AHA!

That's why it's a great new adventure like Mama and Daddy said! It's like I've been on a treasure hunt and I didn't even know what I was looking for!

Then all of a sudden I started finding all of these treasures hidden in all of these different places that are all mine! (Not even with a treasure map, just me and my family— the greatest finders ever!)

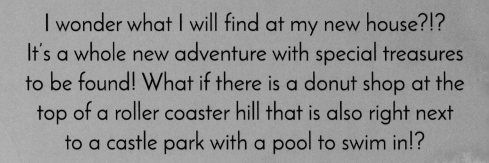

I wonder what I will find at my new house?!?
It's a whole new adventure with special treasures
to be found! What if there is a donut shop at the
top of a roller coaster hill that is also right next
to a castle park with a pool to swim in!?

Or what if everything
is different and new?

Maybe instead of roller coaster hills there will be a desert where you can see everything until forever! Or an ocean with waves as high as the sky! Maybe instead of a castle park, there is a rocket ship slide. And instead of a donut shop, there is an ice cream store where I can get whatever I want!

ICE CREAM

I'll really miss all of those old things, but all of a sudden I'm kind of excited for all of these new treasures I might find!!

I better get packing!! I've got
an adventure to go on with
treasures to find, and new people
to meet, and old friends to keep in
touch with! Maybe moving
(again) isn't so bad after all!!

TREASURES I FOUND AT MY OLD HOME

1. _____

2. _____

3. _____

4. _____

OLD FRIENDS THAT I WILL KEEP IN TOUCH WITH

1. _____

2. _____

3. _____

4. _____

TREASURES I FOUND AT MY NEW HOME

1. _____

2. _____

3. _____

4. _____

NEW FRIENDS I MADE AT MY NEW HOME

1. _____

2. _____

3. _____

4. _____

It's so fun to put a letter in the mail and your friends will be so excited to hear from you!! Start keeping in touch with these fun letter-writing pages!!

Don't forget to ask Mama or Daddy for an envelope and a stamp so it can get sent!!

Dear _____ ,

_____

_____

_____

_____

_____

_____

_____

Your Friend,

_____

Dear _____ ,

_____

_____

_____

_____

_____

_____

_____

Your Friend,

_____

Dear _____ ,

_____

_____

_____

_____

_____

_____

_____

Your Friend,

_____

Made in the USA
Columbia, SC
13 February 2020